This book should be returned to any branch of the
Lancashire County Library on or before the date shown

1 4 AUG 2014		CLE
1 0 OCT 2014		11/3
8/3/16		
− 1 AUG 2017		
− 9 MAY 2019		

First published 2012 by Fast-Print Publishing of
Peterborough, England.

www.fast-print.net/store.php

The Vegetarian Vampire: The Lost Fangs
Copyright © Helen Wendy Cooper 2013

ISBN: 978-178035-651-8

A catalogue record for this book is available from the British Library

An environmentally friendly book printed and bound in England by
www.printondemand-worldwide.com

Mixed Sources
Product group from well-managed
forests, and other controlled sources
www.fsc.org Cert no. TT-COC-002641
© 1996 Forest Stewardship Council
FSC

PEFC Certified
This product is
from sustainably
managed forests
and controlled
sources
www.pefc.org
PEFC
PEFC/16-33-415

This book is made entirely of chain-of-custody materials

In memory of my lovely nan

Margaret Phyllis Cooper.

Collect books by Helen Wendy Cooper

THE VEGETARIAN VAMPIRE – Halloween Disco

SHAPE LAND – Trevor Triangle Loses the Mail

SHAPE LAND – Silly Samuel Square

www.helenwendycooper.co.uk

Contents

– Helen Wendy Cooper –

The Vegetarian Vampire: The Lost Fangs

Chapter 1 - Fangs

"Ouch!" said Vernon, poking his fang. "It's all wobbly!"

"Well don't touch it!" said Mum.

"But it's my FANG!"

Vernon's left fang had been wobbly for two days.

"What can I eat for lunch, Mum?" asked Vernon.

"Nothing chewy, how about tomato soup?" said Mum.

"Ooh, yes please!"

Tomato soup was Vernon's favourite; he always took it in a flask to school.

"Crunchy bread?" asked Mum, smiling.

"No Mum, it'll make my fang bleed!"

The night before, Vernon had had a vegetable burger for tea. He loved vegetable burgers, but when he'd taken a massive bite he'd screamed! Pain shot up his fang and his mouth filled with blood. Yuck, yuck, YUCK!

He'd rushed to the bathroom to be sick.

This morning he didn't dare eat anything, in case his fang fell out.

Vernon went to his bedroom to see Mikey, his pet tarantula. He put some dead grasshoppers into his tank.

"At least you won't be hungry, Mikey," signed Vernon.

After a last look at his fang in the mirror, Vernon set off for school.

Vernon's school was full of bloodsucking vampires, who loved meat and blood.

Vernon hated the sight of blood and he hated the smell of meat.

Vernon was a vegetarian vampire and only his family and friend Veronica knew. It was his biggest secret!

Chapter 2 - The Vampire Tooth Fairy

Vernon arrived at school and ran to his best friend Malcolm.

"Vernon, you've got blood on your chin!" Malcolm said.

"Oh, must be from my fang... it's all wobbly!"

"Are you losing your fangs?" said Malcolm, eyes wide. "Wow, you'll get a visit from the vampire tooth fairy!"

"Who's she?" asked Vernon.

"She's the most important vampire fairy of all," Malcolm whispered, "She will come and collect your fangs from under your pillow, then your new fangs will grow!"

Vernon smiled; at least he'd get some new fangs.

"But if you lose your fangs and the vampire tooth fairy can't collect them, your fangs will never, ever grow back!"

Vernon gasped and quickly touched his wobbly fang.

On the way to class Vernon went to the toilets. He bumped into Big Brian the Bully.

"Oi, Small Fangs, what've you got on your chin?"

"Nothing," said Vernon, looking at his toes.

"That's blood! Can't you eat your breakfast properly, Small Fangs?" asked Big Brian, laughing.

Vernon went to walk away but Big Brian stopped him.

"That blood's coming from your mouth! Ha ha, Vernon's got wobbly fangs! Make sure you don't lose them, because the vampire tooth fairy wouldn't be happy!"

Vernon left the toilets and rushed to class. He began to worry about his fangs, he didn't want to upset the vampire tooth fairy.

At class, Vernon saw Veronica, his new friend. Veronica was just like Vernon, a vegetarian vampire. He was going to her house for tea and Vernon couldn't wait. He soon forgot all about his wobbly fang!

Chapter 3 ~ Burger and Chips

"Vegetable burger and chips?" said Veronica's mum.

"Yes please," said Vernon and Veronica together.

"I'm really hungry!" said Vernon, and opened his mouth wide. He took a big bite of his burger.

"Ooooow!" he cried and quickly closed his mouth.

SNAP... Vernon's fang fell out!

He didn't want Veronica to see, so he quickly put his fang into his coat pocket.

He was still hungry, so he bit into the burger again.

"Arragh!" he said, putting his hand on his cheek.

"Are you alright Vernon?" asked Veronica.

Vernon's face went red and he touched his other fang. It was all wobbly.

He poked it... SNAP!

"Oh no, my other fang has fallen out too!" Vernon said, holding the fang.

"Don't worry Vernon, the vampire tooth fairy will come and you'll get some new fangs!" said Veronica.

Vernon gulped and nodded, eating the rest of his tea. He put the fang with his other one in his pocket.

The next day Vernon soon forgot about his broken fangs as it was the weekend!

On Saturday Vernon's dad took him to the woods where they explored caves and ran up and down muddy banks.

On Sunday he cleaned out Mikey's tank and tidied his room.

Vernon had so much fun, he completely forgot about the broken fangs in his coat pocket.

Chapter 4 - Missing

On Monday morning, Vernon hung up his coat at class. He grinned at Malcolm to show him his missing fangs, they both laughed.

"You lost your fangs then, Small Fangs!" Big Brian shouted from the back of the classroom. "You put them under your pillow?"

"Not yet," mumbled Vernon, looking at his coat pocket.

"I forgot," he whispered to Malcolm.

Mr Coffins arrived at class and began teaching. At break time the whistle blew and all the children rushed to the coat stands; Vernon was last to reach his. He put his coat on and put his hand in his pocket.

"Malcolm, Malcolm, my fangs have gone! I put them in my coat pocket."

"Oh no... but your fangs won't grow back unless you put the old ones under your pillow," said Malcolm.

Vernon's eyes began to fill with tears.

"Don't worry Vernon, we'll find them. We'll have a look after school."

Vernon thought long and hard where they could be. He could have lost them at Veronica's house, his own home, school or even the cave he went in with his dad.

At home time, Vernon found Malcolm.

"Come on Malcolm; let's search my house first. Veronica's going to look in her house."

At Vernon's house, the boys searched everywhere.

"Look at these mouldy crumbs Vernon, yuck!" said Malcolm, looking under the sofa.

"Ooh, smelly!" said Vernon, when he looked behind the toilet.

"Argh, gross!" said Malcolm, when he checked the dustbin.

"I'm going to go home Vernon, I need a bath!" said Malcolm.

Vernon searched his bedroom and Mikey's tank, but he still didn't find his fangs.

"Please don't come tonight, Vampire Tooth Fairy," he whispered, as he climbed into his coffin to go to sleep.

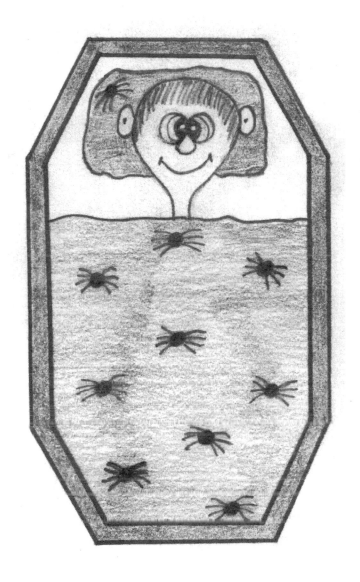

Chapter 5 - The Cave

The next day after school Malcolm and Vernon went to the forest.

"Come on Malcolm, this way," called Vernon, walking between the whispering trees.

"It's a bit muddy," said Malcolm, clinging onto tree branches, to stop himself falling.

"Look Malcolm, look!" said Vernon. "There's the cave!"

Vernon ran to the cave and switched on his torch. It was dark inside and water sparkled on the walls. "It's really smelly in here," said Vernon wrinkling his nose.

"Wow, did your dad bring you here?" Malcolm said, his eyes wide.

"Yes and my fangs might have fallen out down there." Vernon pointed to the sloping floor. The boys shone a torch around the cave.

"This cave is huge!" said Malcolm.

"Helloooooo," he shouted.

"Ssssh" said Vernon, "there might be things living in here... I can't see my fangs anywhere."

"This cave is SPOOKTACKULAR! Look at the slime on the walls," said Malcolm.

"Never mind the slime, what's that noise?" Vernon froze. Suddenly the sound of flapping wings echoed through the cave.

"Bats, Malcolm, vampire bats... quick, RUN!"

Both boys turned around. Slipping and sliding on the rocky floor, they ran out of the cave.

"Phew, we made it," sighed Malcolm.

"No... the bats are coming out of the cave. We've woken them up!"

"ARGH!" Both boys screamed and ran up the muddy banks of the forest.

They didn't stop running until they were both safely home.

Chapter 6 ~ Hidden

The next day the boys met early at school.

"Veronica couldn't find my fangs, they're not at home or in the cave. They must be at school," said Vernon.

"Where shall we look?" asked Malcolm.

"Let's start with the canteen."

They looked under the tables and chairs, behind the curtains, and even in the bins.

"Urgh, rotten meat stinks!" said Vernon, holding his nose.

"Mouldy bread is disgusting!" said Malcolm, looking in the bin.

They searched the classrooms, main hall and playground. There was still no sign of Vernon's fangs.

Other children began to arrive at school.

"Oi Small Fangs, have you found your old fangs yet?" shouted Big Brian the Bully in the play ground. Vernon shook his head and Brian started laughing.

The whistle blew and the boys went to Mr Coffin's classroom.

"How does Brian know I've lost my fangs?" Vernon said, sitting by Malcolm.

"It was Monday I lost my fangs, but what if they were taken out of my coat?"

"By Big Brian?" Malcolm whispered.

"Yes, when everyone rushed to get their coats at playtime," said Vernon.

"But where would he put them?" asked Malcolm.

"In the toilets... he knows I wouldn't look there because they're smelly!"

Vernon smiled, he finally knew where his fangs would be!

Chapter 7 - New Fangs

At break Vernon searched the toilets for his fangs. Malcolm stood guard, holding his nose, looking out for Big Brian.

"I've found them Malcolm, I've found them!" called Vernon, "They were Sellotaped to the bottom of the toilet door."

"Yeah! Hooray!" said Malcolm.

"Yippee!" said Vernon, dancing around the toilet.

Vernon put them safely in his school bag. "I'm not going to lose these again," he said.

That night Vernon placed his fangs under his pillow. He fell asleep in seconds, dreaming of new, white, shiny fangs.

The next day he woke up and jumped out of his coffin. Pulling up his pillow, he found a large silver coin.

"My fangs have gone, yippee! The vampire tooth fairy has been!"

He ran to the bathroom and looked in the mirror. He had two tiny white fangs starting to grow.

"Mum, mum, my new fangs are growing!" he shouted downstairs.

At school, Vernon saw Veronica in the playground.

"Veronica, look I've got my new fangs!" he said.

"FANGTASTIC! You can come to mine for tea again then," she said, smiling.

"Yes, I'd love another veggie burger," he whispered. Being a vegetarian vampire was still his biggest secret.

When Vernon arrived at his class, all the other children were laughing.

"What's happened?" he asked Malcolm.

"Big Brian has lost his fangs!" said Malcolm.

"What?" Vernon's eyes nearly popped out of his head.

"Big Brian's fangs fell out last night, and he doesn't know where he's put them."

Vernon looked over at Big Brian the Bully, who sat with his arms crossed and a red face.

"Hey Brian, you should look in the toilets, someone had put my fangs in there," shouted Vernon smiling.

Big Brian huffed and looked at the floor.

"He never said sorry for hiding your fangs, did he?" asked Malcolm.

"No he didn't, but I will help him look for his later. Just not right now," he said, smiling.

"Today is going to be a GREAT day!" said Vernon, showing Malcolm his new shiny fangs.

About the Author

Helen Wendy Cooper lives in Worcestershire, England, with her boyfriend, three cats, a tortoise, three turtles and four fish.

She thinks writing and drawing for children is fun, fun, fun!

Helen's had a few day jobs too, including being a military musician, a nursery nurse and working for the Police.

Helen started writing children's books for her GCSEs when she was 14 years old.

She hopes you enjoy her stories!

Also available:

The Vegetarian Vampire
Word Search

N	O	N	R	E	V	X	Q	W	N
T	A	R	A	N	T	U	L	A	L
S	Z	F	L	W	Z	Z	I	P	L
G	V	A	M	P	I	R	E	F	S
N	W	Y	Y	Z	A	W	Y	Q	S
A	Z	L	Q	T	P	Z	Q	P	K
F	Q	X	E	Y	D	O	O	L	B
Z	Y	G	Y	M	I	K	E	Y	A
W	E	L	Z	W	F	Z	W	F	T
V	Z	M	A	L	C	O	L	M	S

VAMPIRE   VEGETARIAN   BATS

VERNON   FANGS   MALCOLM

BLOOD   TARANTULA   MIKEY

Creepy crawlies word search

B	E	E	X	K	R	Z	E	D
E	L	T	E	E	B	C	A	R
Y	L	F	D	P	I	K	R	I
I	Q	I	X	L	X	S	W	B
P	P	K	D	W	Z	L	I	Y
S	W	O	A	N	T	U	G	D
A	O	Z	Q	X	Z	G	X	A
W	Z	L	I	A	N	S	Q	L

BEE   WOODLICE   LADYBIRD

WASP   SNAIL   ANT   EARWIG

SPIDER   SLUG   FLY   BEETLE

COMING SOON...

THE VEGETARIAN VAMPIRE:

THE VAMPIRE CAT!